the Trial of the Stone

A folktale retold by Richardo Keens-Douglas

Illustrated by Stéphane Jorisch

Annick Press Ltd.
Toronto/New York/Vancouver

Designed by Andrée Lauzon

Annick Press first published a version of this
story, by Francis Kongani, in Wordsandwich (1975),
under the Books by Kids imprint.

THE CANADA COUNCIL | LE CONSEIL DES ARTS
FOR THE ARTS | DU CANADA
SINCE 1957 | DEPUIS 1957

We acknowledge the support of the Canada
Council for the Arts, the Ontario Arts Council,
and the Government of Canada through the
Book Publishing Industry Development Program
(BPIDP) for our publishing activities.

Cataloguing in Publication Data

Keens-Douglas, Richardo
        The Trial of the stone

ISBN 1-55037-647-0 (bound)   ISBN 1-55037-646-2 (pbk.)

I. Jorisch, Stéphane. II. Title.

PS8571.E44545T74   2000   jC813'.54   C00-930580-7
PZ7.K43T74 2000

The art in this book was rendered in
watercolor, gouache, and pen-and-ink.
The text was typeset in Spectrum.

Distributed in Canada by:
Firefly Books Ltd.
3680 Victoria Park Avenue
Willowdale, ON
M2H 3K1

Published in the U.S.A. by Annick Press (U.S.) Ltd.

Distributed in the U.S.A. by:
Firefly Books (U.S.) Inc.
P.O. Box 1338
Ellicott Station
Buffalo, NY 14205

Printed and bound in Canada by:
Friesens, Altona, Manitoba

visit us at: www.annickpress.com

Thank you, God, for all the blessings you have bestowed upon me—blessings too numerous to mention.

R.K-D.

To Antoine. A penny for your thoughts.

S.J.

A young boy called Matt had been walking on the road all day to visit his grandfather in another village.

Night was falling and he was tired, so he found a place by the side of the road where he could sleep, just outside a small town. He would continue his journey in the morning. In his pocket he carried a few coins. Worried that someone might come and take them while he slept, he hid the coins under a large stone.

Then he lay down under the
moonlit sky and fell asleep.

But Matt was not alone.

The next morning Matt woke up very hungry. He stretched and decided to wash in the nearby stream before going into town to buy a bit of breakfast. When he reached under the stone to find his little treasure, he felt only dry earth.

He pushed the stone aside with great difficulty and looked everywhere, his heart beating fast. These few coins were all the money he possessed in the world. Now Matt began to cry, for the money was gone. He looked under all the stones he could see, but found nothing.

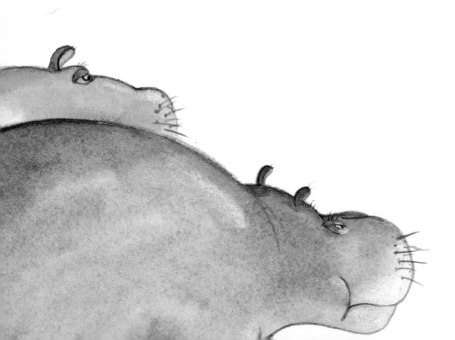

He wailed so loudly that the townspeople came running to see what was wrong, the Chief and the Town Constable among them.

So the boy told his story.

"Did you see anybody before you fell asleep?" asked the Chief.

Matt shook his head.

"Where is this stone?" asked the Chief, and Matt pointed to the place where he had hidden his coins. The Chief scratched his chin. Finally, he held up his hand. "Arrest this stone," he said to the Constable. "It will stand trial for robbery."

No one moved, thinking they must have heard wrong.

"Take it to the court," said the Chief. "What are you waiting for?"

It took three strong men to carry the accused to the court, which was already overflowing with curious people. The Constable calmed the excited crowd, while the stone and the boy stood in front of the Chief.

But before things could get underway, a large family of geese noisily invaded the courtyard and had to be persuaded to leave.

"Stone, do you admit robbing this boy, Matt, of his money?" asked the Chief.

There was no reply.

The Chief then told the clerk to record that the stone refused to answer. A loud laugh came from a man in a red shirt. The Constable gave him a stern look.

"Stone, what were you doing at the edge of the road?" asked the Chief.

The stone did not respond. There was more laughter from the crowd.

"Quiet in the court," said the Chief, and he looked serious. "Stone, what village are you from?" he asked.

The stone did not reply, but a woman in the crowd stuffed her scarf into her mouth to muffle her giggles.

"Stone, who are your parents?" the Chief demanded next.

When the stone remained silent once again, the Chief instructed the clerk to record that the stone showed contempt of court and would be punished. The stone showed no emotion, but at this the crowd burst out laughing. The man in the red shirt toppled right over, he was so amused.

The Chief stood up and shouted to the clerk, "Enter in the records that upon the judgment the crowd raised a huge commotion in disrespect of the court," and right then and there he fined each spectator one penny. The Constable collected the coins and the Chief turned them over to the delighted Matt, who was soon on his way to his grandfather's village, having first enjoyed a fine breakfast.

As for the stone, the man in the red shirt was ordered to take it back to the side of the road all by himself.

The End

Other books by the author

The Nutmeg Princess

La Diablesse and the Baby

Grandpa's Visit

Freedom Child of the Sea

The Miss Meow Pageant